This book belongs to:

_____

_____

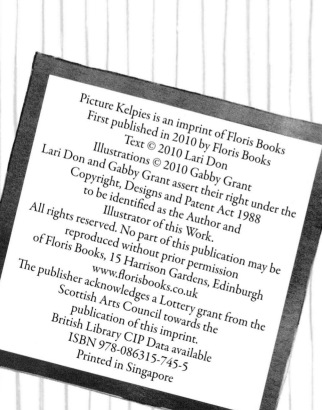

Picture Kelpies is an imprint of Floris Books
First published in 2010 by Floris Books
Text © 2010 Lari Don
Illustrations © 2010 Gabby Grant
Lari Don and Gabby Grant assert their right under the
Copyright, Designs and Patent Act 1988
to be identified as the Author and
Illustrator of this Work.
All rights reserved. No part of this publication may be
reproduced without prior permission
of Floris Books, 15 Harrison Gardens, Edinburgh
www.florisbooks.co.uk
The publisher acknowledges a Lottery grant from the
Scottish Arts Council towards the
publication of this imprint.
British Library CIP Data available
ISBN 978-086315-745-5
Printed in Singapore

Lari Don

The BIG BOTTOM HUNT

Illustrated by
Gabby Grant

Picture Kelpies

On the day of the big bottom hunt, Sandy and Ella went beach-combing. They took a bucket, a net and a magnifying glass.

They walked along the shoreline, looking for treasures and toys washed up by the sea.

Last week, they found a
burst football, one welly and
a crab's pincer.

The week before, they
found an orange hard
hat, three spiral shells
and a stripy stone.

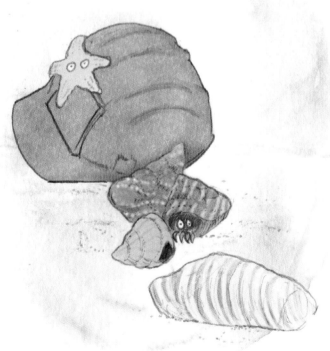

On the day of the big bottom hunt, Sandy saw something glitter by the jaggy rocks.

They ran up to have a look.

It was a telescope.
But it wasn't stained by salt water, or scraped by sand and stones.

"This is too clean and shiny to have been washed up by the sea. It must have been left by a person," said Sandy. "We can't take it home. We'd better find its owner."
"How do we know who to give it back to?" asked Ella.

"Let's look for clues," said Sandy, who
wanted to be a detective when he grew up.
    Beside the telescope they found some
footprints and an odd shape in the sand.
    The footprints were blurry, and Sandy
thought most of them were Ella's, but the
odd shape was …

"A bottom print!" declared Sandy.

"Someone sat here, looking out to sea with their telescope, and they left their bottom print behind them in the sand. We just have to find the person whose bottom fits this shape and we've found the telescope's owner."

"Do we have to get everyone in the village to sit in this wee hole?" asked Ella.

"No, the sand will dry out soon and the bottom print will blow away. We have to PRESERVE THE EVIDENCE!" said Sandy grandly.

So they ran home for some big sheets of paper and their art box, and they traced the bottom print.

Then the big bottom hunt began.

"Is this your bottom?" they asked Miss Forsythe.

"My bottom? How dare you enquire about my bottom? You children may have bottoms, but I am a Forsythe and we have never had bottoms. We have posteriors, or sit upons, or rear ends."

She slammed the door.

"Sorry Miss Forsythe," they sang, and ran off giggling.

"Is this your bottom?" they asked Angus.

"Bottom!" he shouted in delight as they put the paper down on the ground and showed him how to sit on it.

When he stopped wriggling and giggling, they could see lots of bottom print round the edge of his shorts.

"You're too wee. It's not your bottom."

"Is this your bottom?" they asked Captain Christie.

"I don't think so," he said. "Why do you ask?"

They showed him the telescope.

"A spy glass!" he exclaimed. "A very fine one too. I had a spy glass when I sailed the sea. I used it to find treasure islands and enemy ships."

"If my bottom fitted, would I get the spy glass as a prize?"

They put the bottom print on his captain's chair and he sat down. The whole sheet of paper disappeared under his trousers.

"Sorry, Captain Christie. It's not your bottom."

"We're looking for a bottom bigger than Angus's bottom," said Ella, "and smaller than Captain Christie's bottom."
     They asked everyone they knew, "Is this your bottom?" But it wasn't anybody's bottom.

It couldn't be baby Ben, because his nappy made one big splodge on the sand.

It couldn't be Mr Balfour, because the folds of his kilt would make his bottom print stripy.

It couldn't be Sandy and Ella's mum, because she never got a chance to sit down.

By teatime they had asked everyone in the village about
their bottom.

Everyone except the summer visitors in the holiday home by the end of the burn.

"We can't ask complete strangers about their bottoms!" said Ella.

"Why not?" argued Sandy. "They can't be any more offended than Miss Forsythe."

Ella had an idea. "Maybe we should use the spy glass to see if any of them have the right size of bottom."

Through the spy glass they saw a mum, a dad, a wee boy and a big girl, who all had ordinary sized bottoms. So they took a couple of deep breaths, marched up to the door and knocked.

The wee boy answered.

"Is this your bottom?" they asked.

"No," he said. "I still have mine."

He waggled his bottom at them, and closed the door.

They knocked again, and this time the mum answered.

"Excuse us, but is this your bottom?"

"Why do you want to know?"

"We found a telescope on the beach beside this bottom print. If we find the person whose bottom fits, we can give them back their telescope."

"Charmaine!" called the mum, and the big girl, who wasn't really so big, just a bit taller than Sandy, came to the door.

"Is this your bottom?" said Sandy and Ella together.

Charmaine laughed. "It could be." And she sat down on the bottom print.

"It fits!" they all shouted.

"Is this your telescope?"

"That's my grandpa's old spy glass!" Charmaine said happily. "Thank you for finding it! How did you know it was mine?"

So Sandy and Ella told her about the clues on the beach, their day of detective work, and all the bottoms they had seen …

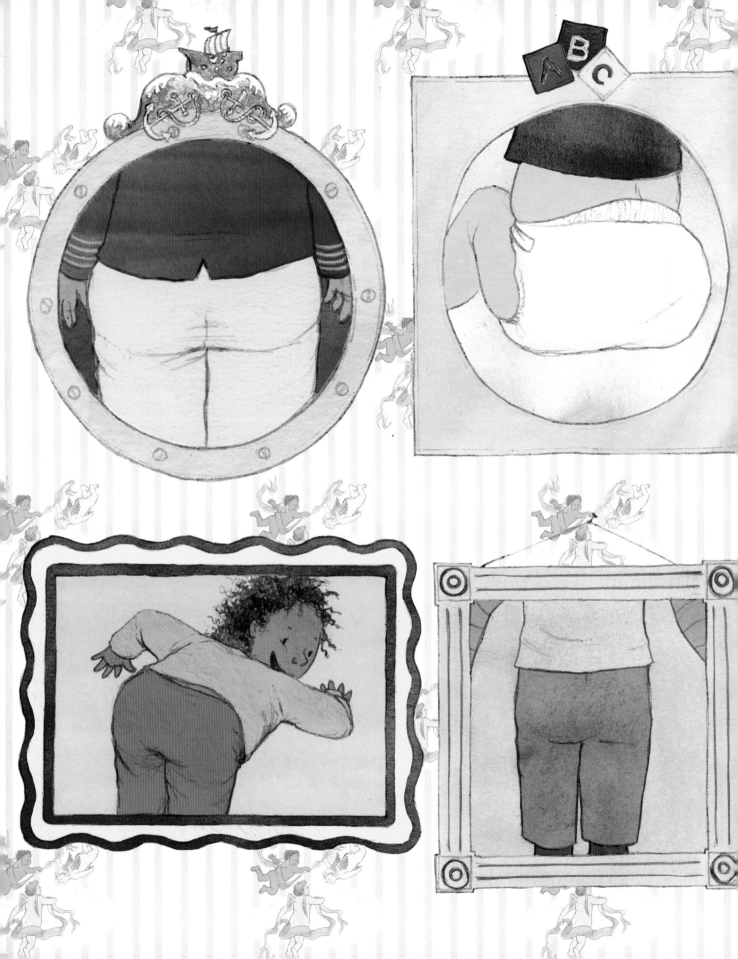

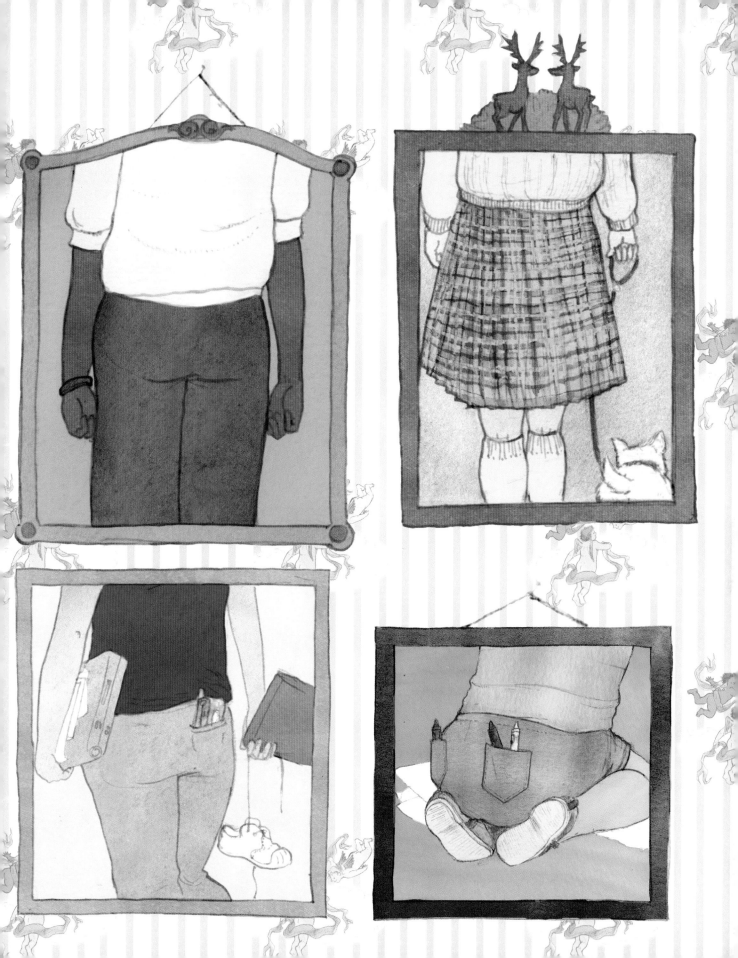

The children met at the beach early the next morning.
They looked out to sea with the spy glass.
They made ...

foot prints

toe prints

hand prints

finger prints

bottom prints

head prints

brother prints

sister prints

... a whole beach full of prints.

And they played happily ever after.
Or at least until the end of the summer holidays.

THE (REAR) END